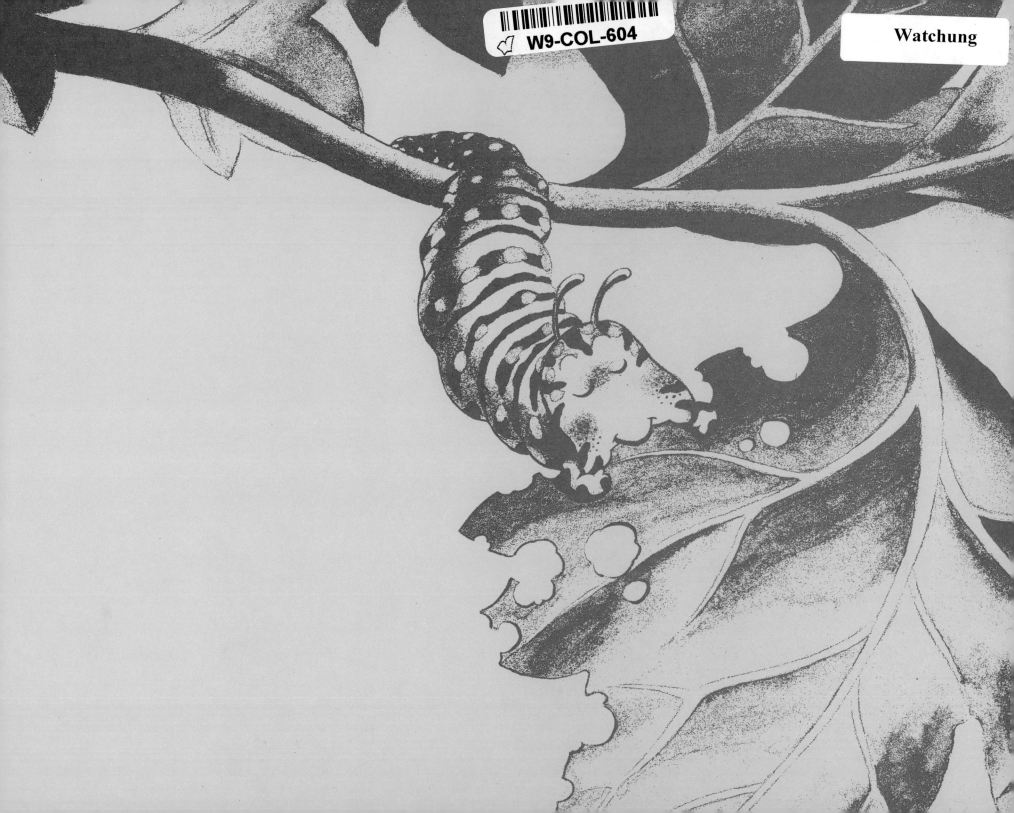

This book is dedicated to embracing the spirit
of positive change.

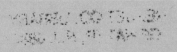

WINGS OF CHANGE

Story by FRANKLIN HILL, Ph.D.

Illustrations by ARIES CHEUNG

PUBLISHING COMPANY, INC.
BELLEVUE, WASHINGTON

"Oh Faith, I just love being a caterpillar," said Anew as they wandered together through the garden. "The morning dew tickles my belly buttons. The afternoon sun warms my fuzzy feet, and these soft green leaves taste so yummy in my tummy. I never want things to change, not one tiny bit!"

Faith, a wise old snail, looked on with a smile. It was time for Anew to learn that changes were in the wind.

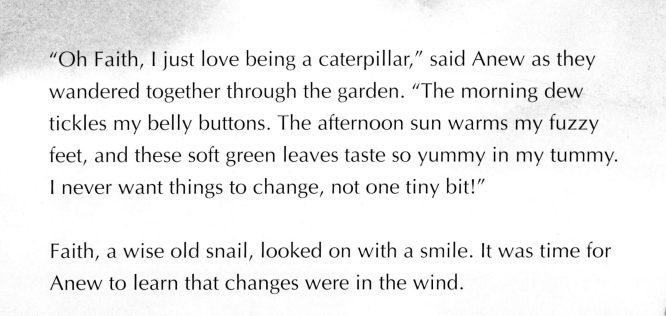

Faith led Anew to a quiet spot in the garden where she could talk and he could listen. Her words painted glowing pictures of the miraculous changes that lay ahead for him. She spoke of brilliant colors, beautiful wings, being able to fly through the air.

Faith then shared a bit of old snail wisdom:

*"As the world turns,
so do you.
When you change for the good,
you change the world, too."*

Anew was very puzzled. He didn't understand what Faith was talking about. How could he ever have wings? He just wanted to stay a happy, little caterpillar.

So, as always, Anew spent the day feeling the dew, smelling the moss, and eating the leaves he loved so much.

That night Anew had a very strange dream.
He was still in a caterpillar's body, but he was
thinking and acting like a butterfly.

In his dream, Anew climbed up a bush, jumped
off a branch, and tried to fly. Luckily, he landed
in a soft puff of moss and had only a few bumps
and bruises. The other caterpillars were shouting,
"Anew, you're acting crazy! Have you
been eating bad leaves?"

When Anew awoke the next morning, he quickly went to tell Faith about his frightening dream.

Knowing that Anew would soon become a butterfly, Faith smiled and gently said, "Butterflies can stand atop rosebuds. They view meadows from the sky. Butterflies hear the echo of the stars.

"So, remember, little one,

"As the world turns,
so do you.
When you change for the good,
you change the world, too."

Anew still didn't understand what
Faith was talking about. So, as always,
he spent the rest of the day as a
happy little caterpillar – feeling the
dew, smelling the moss, and eating
the leaves he loved so much.

That night Anew had another unusual dream.
This time he still had a caterpillar's body, but with
big butterfly wings – so bright, so beautiful,
so brilliant.

In this dream, a strong wind blew Anew off a high
branch and he crashed to the ground. The fragile
wings could not bear the weight of his heavy
caterpillar body.

His heart pounding, Anew awoke from his
frightening dream. Relieved to see that he was still
a caterpillar, he settled peacefully back to sleep.

Later that night, Anew had another dream. Again he had big butterfly wings. But this time his body was very thin and he had six spindly legs. Although he now had the body of a butterfly, Anew was still thinking like a caterpillar. So instead of flying, he was crawling everywhere in search of food, causing his thin legs to become very tired and sore.

In his dream, Anew became frightened when a bird suddenly flew overhead. Still thinking like a caterpillar, he hid under a thorny bush, tearing his fragile wings.

Thinking like a caterpillar does not work for butterflies.

Early the next morning Anew hurried
to tell Faith about his dreams.

Faith was most understanding. "Tonight," she
explained, "you will make a very special bed where
you will sleep in a very special way. From now on
there will be no more bad dreams.

"So remember...

"As the world turns,
so do you.
When you change for the good,
you change the world, too."

As Faith had predicted, that night Anew began to spin a
cocoon. "I don't know why I'm doing this," he thought,
"but it sure feels right."

While Anew spun and spun, he found himself singing,

"As the world turns,
so do you.
When you change for the good,
you change the world, too."

His song made him feel so, so good as he worked long into the night.

Very tired now, Anew slowly snuggled into his new bed. He felt safe and warm.

A special light began to warm him from the inside, too, touching every bit of his caterpillar body. "Ooooh, that tickles," he thought, feeling very peaceful.

Days passed and spring became summer. One fine morning
Anew awoke and began to untangle himself from his cocoon.
"I feel so different," he thought as he worked himself free,
"and I feel so, so happy."

In his heart he heard a soft echo,

"As the world turns,
so do you.
When you change for the good,
you change the world, too."

His new wings gracefully opened, and a gentle breeze lifted Anew into the air. "Look!" he shouted. "I can fly!

"I can stand atop rosebuds and view meadows from the sky. I can hear the echo of the stars. I just love being a butterfly!"

Anew flew higher and higher, singing a new song of faith,

"As the world turns,
so do I.
When I change for the good,
I can touch the sky."

Interactive Guide For Exploring The Topic Of Change

When do you feel like Anew the caterpillar – happy and content, not wanting anything to change?

When are you like Faith the snail – helping someone else?

Who helps you – like Faith helps Anew?

Where do you feel safe and warm – like Anew in his cocoon?

When are you like Anew the butterfly – doing something for the first time and finding it wonderful?

How can you help change the world for the good?

ILLUMINATION
Arts

P.O. Box 1865, Bellevue, WA 98009
Tel: 425-644-7185 ★ 888-210-8216 ★ Fax: 425-644-9274
liteinfo@illumin.com ★ www.illumin.com

Library of Congress Cataloging-in-Publication Data

Hill, Franklin, 1950-
    Wings of change / story by Franklin Hill; illustrations by Aries Cheung.
        p. cm.
    Summary: When Anew, the caterpillar, has nightmares in which he's not ready to be a butterfly, his snail friend, Faith, reassures him.
    ISBN 0-935699-18-X
    [1. Caterpillars–Fiction. 2. Nightmares–Fiction. 3. Butterflies–Fiction. 4. Metamorphosis–Fiction. 5. Snails–Fiction.] I. Cheung, Aries, 1960- ill. II. Title.

PZ7.H5523 Wi 2000
[E]–dc21

        00-058189

Published in the United States of America

Printed by Star Standard Industries in Singapore

Book Designers:
Molly Murrah, Murrah & Company, Kirkland, Washington
Paul Langland, Paul Langland Design, Seattle, Washington

FRANKLIN HILL, PH.D.
Author

Dr. Franklin Hill, once a public school teacher, is now an internationally recognized educational futurist who specializes in planning new facilities. He has consulted in the design of over 250 schools worldwide.

The Disney Development Company chose Dr. Hill to facility-plan the Celebration School near Orlando, Florida. He has served as a consultant with such prominent organizations as IBM and BC Tel of Canada.

Wings of Change presents the story of a contented caterpillar who is afraid to become a butterfly. This simple metaphor reflects the insights Dr. Hill has gained while facilitating progressive changes in education.

Whether he is working with classrooms of children or as a keynote speaker at professional conferences, Franklin Hill uses this story to show how the process of change, though sometimes a bit scary, can lead to positive transformation.

Dr. Hill lives in Bellevue, Washington where he is the father of two teenage sons. Together they enjoy sailing, traveling, gardening, cooking, and other family activities.

ARIES CHEUNG
Illustrator

An award-winning artist who is proficient in a variety of mediums, Aries Cheung chose watercolor to create the exceptionally charming and whimsical illustrations for this book.

Aries' graphic design talents have been utilized by many international companies, including IBM, Kodak, and J. Walter Thompson. His first illustrated book for Illumination Arts, *The Bonsai Bear,* is a unique story set in ancient Japan. This beautiful book was a finalist for the 2000 Children's Book of the Year Award from the Coalition of Visionary Retailers.

Born in Hong Kong, Aries currently resides in Toronto, Canada, where he is active in the performing arts, including classical and modern dance, mime, and acting. Aries is a member of the Canadian Society of Children's Authors, Illustrators and Performers. He frequently contributes his artistic skills to non-profit cultural and health organizations.

Visit the "Wings" website at
www.wingsofchange-thebook.com

THE ILLUMINATION ARTS COLLECTION OF INSPIRING CHILDREN'S BOOKS

THE LITTLE WIZARD

Written and illustrated by Jody Bergsma $15.95, 0-935699-19-8

A young boy discovers a wizard's cloak while on a mission to save his mother's life.

THE DOLL LADY

By H. Elizabeth Collins-Varni, illustrated by Judy Kuusisto $15.95 0-935699-24-4

The Doll Lady tells children to treat dolls kindly and with great love, for they are just like people.

ALL I SEE IS PART OF ME

Winner – 1996 Award of Excellence – Body Mind Spirit Magazine

By Chara Curtis, illustrated by Cynthia Aldrich $15.95, 0-935699-07-4

In this international bestseller, a child finds the light within his heart and his common link with all of life.

THE BONSAI BEAR

Finalist – 2000 Children's Picture Book of the Year – Coalition of Visionary Retailers

By Bernard Libster, illustrated by Aries Cheung $15.95, 0-935699-15-5

Issa uses bonsai methods to keep his pet bear small, but the playful cub dreams of following his true nature.

CORNELIUS AND THE DOG STAR

Winner – 1996 Award of Excellence – Body Mind Spirit Magazine

By Diana Spyropulos, illustrated by Ray Williams $15.95, 0-935699-08-2

Grouchy old Cornelius Basset Hound can't enter Dog Heaven until he learns about love, fun, and kindness.

DRAGON

Winner – 2000 Children's Picture Book of the Year – Coalition of Visionary Retailers

Written and Illustrated by Jody Bergsma $15.95, 0-935699-17-1

Born on the same day, a gentle prince and a fire-breathing dragon share a prophetic destiny.

DREAMBIRDS

1998 Visionary Award for Best Children's Book – Coalition of Visionary Retailers

By David Ogden, illustrated by Jody Bergsma $16.95, 0-935699-09-0

A Native American boy battles his own ego as he searches for the elusive dreambird and its powerful gift.

FUN IS A FEELING

By Chara M. Curtis, illustrated by Cynthia Aldrich $15.95, 0-935699-13-9

Find your fun! "Fun isn't something or somewhere or who. It's a feeling of joy that lives inside of you."

HOW FAR TO HEAVEN

By Chara M. Curtis, illustrated by Cynthia Aldrich $15.95, 0-935699-06-6

Exploring the wonders of nature, Nanna and her granddaughter discover heaven all around them.

THE RIGHT TOUCH

Winner – Benjamin Franklin Parenting Award, Selected as Outstanding by the Parents Council

By Sandy Kleven, LCSW, illustrated by Jody Bergsma $15.95, 0-935699-10-4

This beautifully illustrated read-aloud story teaches children how to prevent sexual abuse.

SKY CASTLE

"Children's Choice for 1999" by Children's Book Council

By Sandra Hanken, illustrated by Jody Bergsma $15.95, 0-935699-14-7

Alive with dolphins, parrots and fairies, this magical tale inspires us to believe in the power of our dreams.

TO SLEEP WITH THE ANGELS

Finalist – 2000 Children's Picture Book of the Year – Coalition of Visionary Retailers

By H. Elizabeth Collins, illustrated by Judy Kuusisto $15.95, 0-935699-16-3

A young girl's guardian Angel comforts her to sleep, filling her dreams with magical adventures.

U.S. Orders: add $2.00 postage; each additional book add $1.00.
Free shipping if ordering 5 or more books.
Washington residents please add 8.6% sales tax.

ILLUMINATION ARTS PUBLISHING COMPANY
1.888.210.8216
425.644.7185 ★ fax: 425.644.9274 ★ P.O. Box 1865, Bellevue, WA 98009
liteinfo@illumin.com ★ www.illumin.com